DESERT RAGE

A Western Adventure

A.T. BUTLER

CHAPTER ONE

Jacob Payne, bounty hunter, had been sitting at the corner table of the San Xavier Cafe all afternoon and was on his fourth cup of coffee. He had been back from his adventure in the town of Haven for five days now, the bulk of which had been spent resting and trying to heal from his bullet wound. But even as worn and incapacitated as he was, Jacob was having a hard time staying put. He was a man who needed action. Healing from a shot to the gut was making him antsy and he had to find a way to force himself to sit still.

Earlier that day he had made his way to the cafe, where Bonnie Loft was waiting tables. She would be there all day and he didn't want to miss a moment with her. Jacob wanted to believe that she'd like to see him, that she was as enamored with spending time with him as he was with her. In the few days since he had been back from his last bounty hunt, they had shared their first kiss but hadn't had much time for anything else. Even conversation was scarce, as she had needed to work. The cafe's other waitress had up and got married and left for the goldfields of California with little warning.

After enough days passed, Jacob had accepted that he would need to be at the cafe as well if he wanted to see her. He could spend time with Bonnie and make himself rest at the same time. He tried to stay out of her way and not distract her from her work. He didn't want to be extra work for her, but simply being in the same room as her had been a balm to his soul.

If he had to rest, he could do it near her.

Near her and near hot food. Better to spend the money sitting at the cafe all day than just getting restless on the porch of his boarding house by himself.

Jacob swallowed down a big mouthful of black coffee and set his empty mug on the wooden table in front of him. Bonnie must have caught that tiny sound. She glanced at him from where she stood near the door, chatting with other patrons. When he caught her eye, she blushed slightly, smiled, and nodded. She'd be over to his table as soon as she could.

Edwin Hogg—Jacob's friend in Tucson and one of his regular poker-playing buddies—entered the cafe. The afternoon light cut into the space through the open door behind him. He paused briefly and looked around before spotting Jacob and making his way to the table.

Without waiting to be invited, Ed sat down across from Jacob, picked up his empty mug, and peered inside.

"Didn't save me none?"

Jacob chuckled. "I'm sure we could even get you your own mug."

"Wow. Living high on the hog, are we?" Ed's voice was as dry as his humor. He turned in his seat to scan the room and tried to get Bonnie's attention.

She had just cleared empty plates and silverware from the two tables closest to the kitchen. Her arms were full and her focus was on taking care of the other diners, but even in her distraction she chanced a glance back to the corner of the room. To Jacob.

Ed had his hand raised to get her to notice him, but she looked right past him to where Jacob Payne sat, smiling softly at her.

A wide smile broke over Bonnie's face. Her

dark, almost black, straight hair was pulled back from her face in a low bun, but a strand had escaped. It hung down in front of her right eye, and since her hands were full of dirty dishes, she was helpless to move it out of her way. She blew a small breath, up and out of the side of her mouth. The strand waved a bit, but then resettled in the same place, directly in front of her eye.

Bonnie and Jacob both laughed—she at her helplessness and he at her endearing habit. She ducked her head briefly before she turned and made her way to the kitchen to drop off her burden.

"She'll come back," Jacob said to his tablemate.

"She didn't even look at me."

"She looked at me, though."

Jacob wrapped his fingers around his empty mug and looked into it, averting his eyes from whatever knowledgeable or mocking expression Ed might have on his face. He'd give him a chance to compose himself. When he looked back up at his friend, the other had exactly the knowing smirk Jacob had expected.

"What?"

"Nothin'," Ed said, and grinned wider. "How you been gettin' on with that injury?"

"Oh." Jacob shrugged. "This? Not bad. I've had worse. Hurts, though."

He put his hand to his side where the outlaw Seamus Maloney had shot him just a few days earlier. The bullet had been removed, but the muscle was still torn and healing. It had been an intense couple days of chasing down the outlaw—the thief and murderer—and the gunshot barely scratched the surface of it. Jacob got his man, but at a steep price.

When he had finally cornered Maloney, the outlaw had insisted he would not be taken alive. Jacob had given him every chance, but in the end he had killed Maloney in a quick draw. He had been well within his rights and within the law to do so. The bounty he had pursued very clearly allowed for the man to be taken in dead if necessary. All the same, it had been the first time Jacob had had to kill a man when bringing him to justice. That experience weighed on him even more than the bullet wound.

He turned his attention back to Ed. "Hurts," he repeated. "But manageable."

"Anyone in particular been helping you manage it?"

"Why don't you just come out and say what you want to say, Ed," Jacob challenged.

The other man opened his mouth, but

closed it again abruptly as rapid footsteps approached their table.

"Good afternoon, gentlemen," Bonnie said as she approached, tucking that one rebellious strand of hair behind her ear. "A refill, Jacob? And what can I get you, Mr. Hogg?"

"Afternoon, Miss Loft," Ed said.

Jacob noted how his smile to greet her held none of the mocking with which he had needled Jacob. Ed liked and respected Bonnie. Heck, everyone liked and respected Bonnie. Tucson was one of the fastest growing cities in the Arizona Territory, and yet every man, woman, and child who met her had only good things to say about her.

Still, she continued to give Jacob her undivided attention. It was enough to make a man nearly burst with pride.

"You hungry, Ed? Or just some coffee for you?"

"Both, if you have it, Bonnie. What's on the menu?"

"We've still got some rabbit stew and I think a bit of the short ribs."

"The ribs'll do. Sounds good. And coffee. And another cup for my friend here," Ed said, gesturing to Jacob. "Maybe you've heard of him. Jacob Payne, famous bounty hunter."

"All right," Jacob said, trying to quiet the man. No part of his job did he do for the attention, but he had been successful enough recently that word couldn't help but spread.

"Mrs. Everill is finishing up an apple pie right now, Jacob. Can I bring you a piece?"

"Yes. Please."

"And coffee?" she asked, not taking her eyes off him.

"And coffee." He nodded. "Thank you."

"Sure thing, gentlemen." Bonnie rested her hand on the tabletop briefly, only an inch or less from Jacob's hand, before turning away to return to the kitchen.

Jacob watched her walk away. It was a full twenty seconds before he realized Ed was talking to him.

"I'm sorry, what was that?"

Ed laughed, loudly enough that the table next to them glanced over.

"Nothin', Jacob," he said, still chuckling. "Don't you mind me none. I know my charms are nothing compared to Miss Loft's."

"All right, then," Jacob agreed with a smile. "What're you doing here anyway, Ed? You know you're not gonna drag me to a game right now."

"No, no. Not that. Not today, anyway," he said. "I was just wondering how long you're gonna be in town this stretch. If you had any leads to jump on right away."

"Not yet," Jacob said. "But you know I never know when something will come up. I promised myself I'd give myself a chance to rest this time. This bullet wound is only going to slow me down if I start up again too soon."

"So how are you filling your time?"

"Like this," Jacob answered. "Sitting for once. Reading the paper. Watching people. Making friends with my neighbors before I'm out on the road again."

"How long do you think you'll be here?"

"Hard to say. At the moment, I have enough saved that I don't have to start thinking about another job for a while yet. And, of course, I'm not as young as I once was, so my healing might take a bit longer."

Ed laughed at that. "That reminds me of the war. We were marching for days with blisters and bullet wounds and aching muscles. But we were all twenty years old, so we thought nothing of it. Remember that?"

"Now that I'm over thirty, seems everything takes a lot longer, doesn't it?"

Ed laughed again, and then they heard delicate footsteps returning to their corner of the cafe.

Two coffee mugs were placed gently on the table, right in between them. "Here you go, gentlemen," Bonnie said. She had managed to carry both of their plates at the same time, and served each man in turn. Pie for Jacob; ribs for Ed. "I'll come back and see about you in a bit."

"Thank you," Jacob said softly.

"This looks mighty tasty, Miss Loft," Ed said. "Give my compliments to the cook."

"I'll do that," she said with a smile and one final look at Jacob, then hurried off to greet the group of older men that had just entered the cafe.

"Seems like you got a pretty good deal set up, Jacob," Ed said as he picked up his fork. He nodded at the fresh, hot apple pie sitting in front of the other man. "Can't really beat that."

"You've got that right," Jacob said as he watched her walk away.

CHAPTER TWO

The two men sat in companionable silence for several minutes, each enjoying the food in front of him. For Jacob's part, he couldn't recall the last time he had allowed himself such a thorough rest, and it had only been a handful of days. He had grown up helping run a large farm in Virginia; the only time he had been permitted more than a day off from his chores was once for a couple weeks when he was twelve. And that was only because his leg had been broken. But his mother had found him tasks to do while sitting in short order. He had been active all throughout the war and then not long after had headed west to Arizona. At every step, Jacob had had to be on the road or be ready to act at a moment's notice.

Now that he had found his vocation taking short-term contracts, he had more control over his time and over what was asked of him. Despite this autonomy, Jacob had yet to actually rest. Truth be told, though, part of that was his own need to keep busy and look out for other people. The last time he tried to take a break he had found himself the leader of a posse to rescue a kidnapped girl. If *he* hadn't done it, it wouldn't have gotten done and Jacob wasn't about to let that girl suffer.

Now that he was actively making himself ignore the wanted posters sitting in the marshal's office, he realized how bad he was at taking breaks. Sitting in the San Xavier Cafe eating fresh apple pie was a luxury he had not looked to have any time soon.

As this thought passed through his mind, the door to the cafe opened again and U.S. Marshal Owen Santos entered. He paused in the doorway briefly to look around, before crossing the room and sitting at the table between Jacob and Ed.

"Marshal," Jacob said, nodding briefly. "You didn't come looking for me, did you?"

"Maybe he just heard about the fresh apple pie," Ed said.

"I did come looking for you, Payne," Santos

replied, ignoring Ed. "It surprised me a bit to learn you were spending your days sitting indoors and sipping coffee. Surprised you don't have your feet up."

"And chatting up Bonnie Loft," Ed interjected.

"Is this a social call or business?" Jacob asked, also ignoring Ed. "Seems I only ever see you when you need my help." He grinned.

"Depends," Santos said. "How's the hole in your side?"

"Hurts," Jacob answered. "I'd rather not be lifting any furniture or breaking in stallions, if I can help it. But it's healing. Why?"

"Think you'd be up to be back-up for me and the deputies? Now, before you answer"—Santos put his hands up to forestall any protest—"just know that you'd be the fourth man in the group. I won't ask you to lead a charge or anything, but I need another gun."

Jacob was saved the need to respond right away by the appearance of Bonnie at the marshal's elbow. It was a testament to how much he had been focused on the man's request that Jacob didn't even realize she was coming to their side of the room.

"Afternoon, Marshal," Bonnie said. "You

hear about the pie that Mrs. Everill cooked up? I still have a few fresh pieces."

"Thank you, ma'am," Santos said. "A piece of pie sounds just about perfect."

She nodded, smiled at Jacob, and left the men to their discussion.

"You didn't come here for the pie," Jacob said quietly.

"No, I came here for the best bounty hunter in five territories."

"Only five?" Ed joked.

As his two companions laughed together, Jacob took a long, slow breath, thinking. He had been telling the truth about the wound still hurting. But he also knew he had done far more work with far worse injuries. If the marshal needed him he would have to at least consider it. Rest or no rest.

"Tell me what you need."

"We're leaving tomorrow morning—"

"I'm not say yes, yet, you understand, Marshal. I just want to know more about it."

Santos paused before he responded, as though weighing his words. "I understand. Here's the basic information. About a day's ride away in Olmos, there's going to be a bank robbery."

"And they invited you to come? Be the lookout, or what?" Ed interjected.

Santos glared at him before continuing. "I'm sure it won't surprise you to learn it is the Slippery Stone Gang that's planning on hitting the bank. Stone has been laying low for months, so it seems about right that we'd be hearing from them now."

"Where's this information from?"

"One of their girls. Got arrested for petty theft in Phoenix and spilled everything to try to talk her way out of it. The sheriff there tells me there is every reason to believe she's telling the truth."

"And you have a plan? Do you know where they are?"

"We're going to draw them out. Lay a trap for them. By my estimation we should be in and out in a day or two, bringing the guilty parties to justice. But, like I said, I need another gun."

Footsteps again interrupted their conversation as Bonnie arrived with the marshal's pie.

"This is the last piece, Marshal. Mrs. Everill is starting on a second one now if you all are still here when it's done."

"Thank you kindly, Miss Loft," Santos said.

Bonnie paused at the edge of the table, just next to Jacob. He glanced up at her and met her eyes. It was clear she had something she wanted to say, but hesitated in front of the other men.

"I don't mean to interrupt," she said hesitatingly. "I just have a quick question . . . Jacob, do you think you'll be able to escort me to church tomorrow?"

Jacob smiled at her, but tore his eyes away to look at Santos. The man held his gaze, pleading almost. Today was Saturday. If Santos wanted to leave the next day for a full days' ride away, there's no way Jacob would be around to go to church with her.

He had to make a decision.

Jacob took a deep breath and looked back to Bonnie.

"I'm sorry," he said softly, "but it seems like the marshal needs my help."

"Again?" she asked. It was more in the tone of surprise than anything else. "Oh. Okay. I understand." She smiled brightly at him. "Try to come back from this one without any new holes in you, though."

"I'll do my best."

He appreciated her calmness and equanimity in the face of his dangerous job, especially considering how he had come home from the last one. With as much as he was on the road and in the line of fire every week, Jacob would need a woman who could be a support to him. He needed a woman who would be understanding about what needed to be done, rather than anxious about what might happen. Bonnie hadn't yet had a full test of her mettle, but with every bounty that Jacob went after, every outlaw he tried to stop, she had more and more chances to show her true colors.

And every time she was just as calm and unruffled as Jacob himself was.

She could be an ideal partner for him.

Bonnie checked in with the other men at the table, making sure they had what they needed, before touching Jacob lightly on the forearm, smiling again and making her way back to the kitchen.

"Did I hear that right, Payne?" Santos asked. "Will you be coming along with me and the boys tomorrow?"

"I'm the fourth man, right?" he clarified. "With this injury, I can't guarantee I'll be any good to you at all, but I can ride a horse and hold a gun well enough. Probably even shoot straight."

"Fifth man, actually, if the sheriff of Olmos doesn't have his hands full with other trouble. You have my word, Jacob. I'll go as easy on you as I can go, but having a man of your temperament and skill along will be just the thing we need to ensure the whole thing goes off without a hitch."

"All right. I'm there. What do I need to know?"

"Bring gear for a few days and meet me in front of my office at dawn. I'll take care of everything."

CHAPTER THREE

The following morning, Jacob was up well before dawn. The marshal had apologized for asking him to leave home and travel on a Sunday, but the bounty hunter knew that justice never slept. It was far more important that they avert the disaster waiting the First Bank of Olmos than they observe the Sabbath. God would understand.

So, accordingly, early Sunday morning, Jacob had all his supplies packed. His horse could be made ready quickly, but he wasn't quite prepared to leave town just yet. He needed to say a better good-bye to Bonnie. True, she was understanding and accommodating—more so than he could have even hoped for. But that didn't mean she deserved to be left behind without a word.

Using his shaving kit as a makeshift desk on his knee, Jacob scrawled out a note to her. After the first couple sentences, apologizing for having to leave and wishing her a pleasant few days, Jacob was at a loss for how to proceed. How much should he say to her? How committed was he to their future together? How much did he want to promise?

After sitting for several minutes without coming up with anything brilliant, Jacob decided that would have to be enough. He had never been good in writing anyway. He had always said the words that he had in the moment. Whatever he had in his heart to say could wait until he came back safely to her and he could tell her in person.

He folded up the note and realized he didn't have an envelope. Instead he simply wrote her name on the outside of the folded paper and was thankful he hadn't written anything more personal in the note. There was no possible way that her landlady Mrs. Withers would find the note on the front porch unsealed and not read it for herself. Given that Mrs. Withers didn't like him much, Jacob would just count it fortunate if she even deigned to give the note to Bonnie at all.

He had just enough time to stop by her boarding house and tuck the note between the door and the doorframe before meeting the marshal. That would have to be good enough. She would understand. She always understood. And he could say more about how he felt when he came home to her.

That set off a train of thought as Jacob made his way to the center of town to meet with Santos and the deputies. He had a few minutes before dawn. In those short moments the idea of having a home to come to, a place where Bonnie was waiting for him, consumed him. A place that had warmth, love and maybe a dog, a home so very different from the boarding house in which he was now living.

He would have to give this idea more thought. His wife had only died a year previously, not long before he left Virginia, and he wasn't sure he was ready to think about anyone taking her place.

But if anyone could fill the place of Louisa, it was Bonnie Loft.

This thought put a relaxed smile on his face as he made his way to the marshal.

"Morning, Payne," Santos called across the

empty street where he and Deputy Lowry stood
jawing by their horses. "We get going now, we'll
be in Olmos by supper."

Deputy Little arrived a moment later and
soon all four of the men were on the trail north
to Olmos. Over the several hours they spent
riding together, breaking for a midday meal and
to water the horses, Jacob kept his mouth shut.
He was plenty happy to listen to the other men
plan and plot and stay out of it himself. The
bounty hunter had agreed to come along with
Santos with the strict understanding that he'd
be an extra gun, no other responsibility
required. When the deputies and the marshal
got to talking about how they would handle the
outlaws and what kind of trap they would be
setting, Jacob stayed out of it. He could take
direction just fine.

Even though he had plenty of ideas and
questioned the timeline of Deputy Little's plan,
that wasn't Jacob's job. That was not what he
was here for. He resolved to do what was asked
of him, and let his wound heal so he could be of
more use in the future.

True to Santos's prediction, the four men
rode into the town of Olmos about supper time.
This late in the year it was after dark and they
had only the illumination coming through the

saloon, hotel and jail windows to light their way. Every other business was closed for the day or off the main street.

The dark, imposing structure of the First Bank of Olmos stood just across the street from the Ferguson Hotel, where the marshal led them.

"This is perfect," Santos said standing in the street and looking up at the hotel. "I'll make sure we get those rooms facing the front, and we can post lookouts right there."

Jacob glanced up at the front of the building. Those rooms would have the perfect view of the bank, but also potentially be right in the line of sight for anyone in the street who thought to look. But, he reminded himself, it was not for him to judge or decide. Jacob was merely there to follow orders.

Santos led the way into the hotel. The counter was deserted, but as he cleared his throat and stepped heavily on the wooden floor, the round, mustached face of an otherwise baby-faced young man trying to make himself look older appeared in the doorway to the back of the room.

"Evening," he said pompously. "Can I help you gentlemen? Looking for a room?"

Santos flashed his badge. "You certainly can.

U.S. Marshal. From Tucson. We're going to need two rooms at least. Four beds. Front of the house so we can overlook the street."

"I'm sorry, sir, but—"

"I don't care what you have to tell the people already in those rooms. Your sheriff will back me up."

"I . . . But—" The young man stammered helplessly for another moment, looking from one man to another as though one of Santos's companions would help him.

"What's your name, son?" Santos asked, more gently this time.

"W. Henry Ferguson," the young man said, standing to his full height and thrusting out his chest like a barnyard cock. "This is my hotel and I can't be turning out my patrons at this time of night. I'm sure you understand."

"And I'm sure you understand that interfering with the doling out of justice is enough cause for me to arrest you as well," Santos replied serenely. "Or maybe you're in league with the perpetrators. If you're not going to aid a U.S. Marshal in the simple task of hospitality, maybe instead you can direct me to the Olmos jail?"

Ferguson cleared his throat nervously and adjusted his tie. "No." His voice cracked. He cleared his throat again. "No, sir. That— That is I surely can direct you there, but there's no need for any talk of arrest. I'll . . . Give me just a few moments, Marshal, and I'll see what I can do."

When he left the four men alone, Santos beckoned them closer.

"We'll finalize the plan tonight. Now that I see the layout of this street and the distances we are dealing with I've got some ideas."

"Will we have time to make adjustments?" Jacob asked.

He peered out through the front window of the hotel into the street. The street seemed narrow enough that they should be able to control the flow and access to the building. That was just a guess, though. From this distance he could make out the shape of the bank building, but no details. It was far too dark.

"Stone's girl said the plan was to attack on Tuesday. The stagecoach leaves early Wednesday morning to take the bags of cash back east to the shareholders offices, so we can expect Stone to attack by the end of the day Tuesday. He'll surely want to wait as long as possible for as much dinero as he can get his hands on."

The deputies nodded.

"So we got all day tomorrow to get our plan in place?" Lowry asked.

"That's right. And we won't want to waste a minute. Just in case he hits the bank early."

Jacob hoped that the marshal's information was correct. Elliott "Slippery" Stone was no greenhorn. If he even had a hint of their presence, he'd slip away without a sign. Arriving in town after dark should help their presence there stay quiet, though Jacob doubted the wisdom of throwing patrons out of their rooms. All that would do is draw more attention to them.

"We'll have time," Santos continued. "It's not like you boys are going to be up drinking on a Sunday night anyway, right? We'll get some grub and head to bed. Tomorrow morning you all better be ready to hit the streets first thing."

Ferguson returned to the hotel counter at that moment and cleared his throat again.

"Well?" Santos said without preamble.

"Yes, sir. I, uh . . . The rooms you requested are empty for you now. Number three and four upstairs. Can I show—"

"No," Santos, interrupting. "We'll be fine."

Jacob followed the marshal and the deputies

up to their hotel rooms. If he were running the show, things would be handled differently. But, he reminded himself, he wasn't. He was just another pair of hands. He kept his mouth shut and made his way to his room.

CHAPTER FOUR

Jacob blinked into the dark room. He felt like he had only just fallen asleep after the full day's ride. As he slowly came to consciousness, the memory of the day before came back to him. The snores of Deputy Little nearby were not enough to wake him, and yet Jacob lay in his bed wide awake anyway. It was still predawn, early enough that there was no light to be had anywhere, no business with lit windows, no gleam of sunlight coming over the horizon.

Jacob sat up in bed, putting his stockinged feet on the wooden floor quietly so as not to disturb the deputy. He rubbed the sleep from his eyes. As he began to wake, the bounty hunter became conscious of his heart pounding. He couldn't go back to sleep now if he tried. If it weren't for the fact that he knew it would be bad for his still-healing wound, he could chase down an outlaw this very moment.

And this was in spite of the fact that it seemed to be the middle of the night. His pocket watch sat on the bureau on the other side of the room, but it would be too dark to see the clock face anyway. Whatever time it was, Jacob knew he was up for the day. As the deputy continued to snore lightly, Jacob felt around the room blindly for his trousers, boots and other belongings. At one point he accidentally ran into the footboard of Little's bed—the deputy jolted, turned over, and settled again into his steady sleep.

Jacob found the door to their room, crept out and down the stairs. A warm, dim light led the way. Someone had lit a lamp in the office.

When he crossed the threshold into that front room, Jacob noticed W. Henry Ferguson hunched over the counter. He sat on a tall stool with a ledger book open in front of him, with a pencil in hand and another two sitting next to him. Leaning on one elbow, Ferguson absent-mindedly gnawed on his fingernails and pored over the contents of the book in front of him.

Jacob cleared his throat.

"Wha—" Ferguson said with a start. He

stood up from his stool and looked around frantically, his eyes resting on Jacob's tall frame in the doorway. Jacob could see the moment he recognized him—the young man stood up taller and puffed his chest out. "Mister . . . Deputy? What can I do for you, sir? I hope your room is to your liking."

Jacob heard the sarcastic bite in his tone and elected to ignore it. Likely the boy didn't intend rudeness, but had just been surprised.

"It is. Just couldn't sleep." Jacob pulled out his pocket watch now that he could see it. "Four o'clock, huh? Are you always up this early in the morning?"

Ferguson remained standing at attention, watching Jacob warily. "I am, sir. Is that a problem?"

Jacob shrugged. "No. Not a problem. Just glad to not be alone this early, I guess."

Ferguson didn't respond. The two men regarded each other for another quiet moment before Jacob tried again.

"I don't suppose there's anywhere around here I could get some coffee, is there? Or do I need to wait another hour or two for your cook? Or, if you've got an apron I suppose I could rustle something up myself."

Ferguson chuckled. Jacob thought to himself

that if the young man stopped taking himself so seriously he might leave a better impression on his guests.

"I can help you with that," Ferguson said, closing the ledger book and tucking it under the counter. "Follow me."

Jacob grinned and happily followed the man who would set him up with a cup of hot coffee.

"What's your name again, deputy?" Ferguson asked over his shoulder. He led Jacob through one doorway, a tiny hallway, and then a second doorway until they had entered the dark dining room of the saloon.

"I'm not a deputy. Just a bounty hunter. Name's Jacob Payne. I work with the marshal quite a bit, and he needed another gun on this job."

"A bounty hunter?" Ferguson stopped and turned to look Jacob up and down. "You kill a lot of men, then, Mr. Payne?"

Jacob flinched inwardly. It had been a point of pride that he had not once brought an outlaw in dead, but that streak had ended just a few days earlier.

"No. I don't," he replied coldly. "Just one in this line of work."

"Only one?"

"Only one," Jacob confirmed.

Ferguson nodded and continued their path through the dining room to the small kitchen behind the bar. At this time of morning the tabletops were mostly clear and waiting for their master to come settle in for the day.

"Seamus Maloney," Jacob said. Now that the subject had been breached he couldn't stop thinking about it. "He had robbed a stage-coach and murdered seven of the people on board."

"Goodness," Ferguson said. He set about to build the fire and heat up water while Jacob stood in the doorway and continued his remi-niscence.

"I went after him. He had to meet his justice, you understand. When I found him, I gave him every chance," he said sorrowfully. "But some men just can't—or won't—make the choice to preserve their own life. It was either kill him or be killed myself."

"Is he the one that gave you that gut shot?" Ferguson asked.

Jacob sighed and nodded. "Seamus Maloney. I'll never forget that name as long as I live."

"I'm sure getting that man out of the public is the best thing to happen for all of us. He sounds like a real bad guy."

"You're right," Jacob said. "It was for the

best. I just sure wish it could have happened differently."

After a short respectful moment of silence, Ferguson cleared his throat again. "Mr. Payne the coffee will be ready shortly. You wanna go find yourself a seat out there? You don't have to wait in here."

Jacob had only been seated for a moment when he heard footsteps coming toward the dining room through the hallway leading back to the hotel. Firm, heavy boots sounded on the wooden floor. Jacob looked up to see U.S. Marshal Owen Santos enter. With just the two of them in the otherwise empty room, the marshal made a beeline for the bounty hunter.

"I thought I heard voices," he said. "Glad to see you're already up, Payne."

"Couldn't sleep," Jacob said. "You too?"

Santos pulled out a chair opposite Jacob and sat. "We've got a lot to do and I don't want to risk missing this chance to nab Stone." He sounded more bitter than Jacob had ever heard him. "He's slipped through my fingers more than any other."

"We'll get him, Marshal."

"We'd better. He's been evading me for more than a year already."

"What's his story?"

Santos shrugged. "Who knows. First I heard of him was in a telegram from the sheriff in St. Louis warning me that he was headed this way. I've picked up a few things here and there from when we've captured members of his gang, but I don't know how much of it is true. Some even seems to contradict the others. But the best I can tell, he was on his way to Oregon but lost his family somehow around Missouri, before they got much farther."

"And then he just . . . what? Started robbing banks and killing people?" Jacob glanced toward the kitchen. The sharp aroma of coffee was beginning to fill the air.

"Robbing banks, yes. I don't know when the murders started, although, now that you mention it I'm not sure I've ever heard of Stone himself killing someone. Everything that can be pinned on him specifically is the thieving."

"Doesn't mean he's not responsible."

"You've got that right," Santos agreed. "Which is why we gotta get him. This is our best chance, Payne."

"We'll get him, Marshal," Jacob assured him.

Ferguson entered, carrying three mugs of steaming coffee. Jacob stood to help him, taking one of the drinks.

"Good morning, Marshal," he said. "Sorry

this is all I have for you. I'm afraid I'm a poor cook. But Fitz should be here soon, I imagine, and we can get you set up with breakfast. Gotta keep you fed if you're gonna be protecting the town, I imagine."

"Thank you," Santos said gruffly.

"I hope I'm not being presumptuous," Ferguson ventured, "but I overheard you talking about Elliott Stone. The Slippery Stone Gang? You expect them here?"

The young man seemed to be valiantly striving to hide the fear in his voice.

"You don't have to worry about a thing," Santos assured him. He blew on his coffee to cool it before continuing. "You just give me the access I need and we'll have no problem."

"Are the rooms satisfactory, then?"

"They are."

"Well, Marshal, whatever you need, just let me know," Ferguson said importantly. "In fact, if I may be so bold . . ."

Jacob and Santos exchanged an amused look. For someone who gave them such trouble the previous evening, the young man seemed mighty inclined to ingratiate himself to them now.

"What's that, Mr. Ferguson?" Jacob said.

"You might try to talk to Fitz when he gets

here. I don't know his full story, only that he has had some experience with Stone's gang. Any insight or understanding you can get here in town, he can at least point the way."

"That's a good tip," Jacob said. "We'll do that."

Santos took a drink of his coffee, made a face, then drank down several more gulps. "I'm gonna go wake the other boys," he said, standing. "Payne, you stay here and talk to Fitz when he's in, will you? The deputies and me'll get to work on the perimeter around the bank."

"I can do that, Marshal," Jacob said with a nod. "And don't worry about Stone. He's as good as yours."

Santos nodded shortly and strode away. They heard his boots clomp up the stairs. Ferguson winced, and Jacob wondered how much the other guests of the hotel would be able to hear that.

"Do you really think you'll get him?" the hotel proprietor asked quietly. "Stone hasn't been caught yet, you know. By anyone."

"I think this is a good chance," Jacob allowed. "We've got a head start on him and a good team assembled. And we'll be sure to get more information. Tell me more about Fitz."

"He only started here a few months ago,"

Ferguson said, sipping his coffee. "He's the best cook we've had in Olmos for a long while. I heard he was Stone's personal cook before they got in a fight over a girl."

"What kind of man is he?"

Ferguson took another sip; Jacob suspected he was stalling for time.

"He's . . . well, he's the kind of man you want to be careful with, I'd say."

The young man was spared making any further definite statements by the arrival of another man in the dining room. He entered through the front door, and as Jacob looked up he realized they must be getting close to time for the saloon to open.

"Mr. Fitzgerald," Ferguson said, standing to greet the newcomer. "I've got a man here who wants to talk to you."

CHAPTER FIVE

Jacob stood to greet Mr. Fitzgerald—Fitz—as he entered the dining room. He had never seen a man like this. He was built like a buffalo: enormously broad across the shoulders, wide in the torso, but narrowed down to impossibly thin legs. And seemed to be covered all over in hair. His thick brown beard and hair both fell halfway down his abdomen.

He scratched at his chest under his beard as he crossed the room to them.

"I keep telling you," he bellowed, "call me Fitz. The mister makes me itchy."

He offered his enormous hand to Jacob, looking him up and down as they shook. Jacob had rare occasion to meet a man bigger than he was, but this Fitz character was a mountain.

"Jacob Payne," he said. "In town with the marshal from Tucson. I have some questions for you, if you have a minute."

"Well, I don't," the big man said matter-of-factly. "Unless you want to roll up your sleeves and start chopping onions. I got work that needs doing. You can do it with me and we'll talk, or you can go about your business."

Jacob grinned at the man's candidness. "I can chop onions. Put me to work, sir."

"Sir makes me itchy too," Fitz said over his shoulder as he strode past Jacob into the kitchen. "It's just Fitz."

"Thanks for the coffee," Jacob said to Ferguson as he followed the cook into the kitchen.

The moment they crossed into the small room, the other man seized two of the largest knives in sight, spun around and threatened the bounty hunter with impalement on one or both of the sharp tips.

"What do you want?"

Jacob instinctively put his hands up, and racked his brain for any mention or hint of a known outlaw that matched Fitz's description. He didn't fear for his life quite yet, but wondered how cautious he should be.

"I'm looking for some information and Mr. Ferguson suggested you might be able to help," Jacob said slowly, soothingly as though trying to calm a wild animal. "That's all I want. Just information."

"About what?" Fitz demanded.

"What you might know about . . . Elliott Stone."

"Slippery?" Fitz asked, scornfully. He lowered the knives. "Yeah, I can tell you some about him. What do you want to know?"

Jacob hesitated, not knowing where to start.

"Mr. Ferguson gave me the impression you were a cook for Stone for a time. Is that right? Do anything else for that man or his gang?"

"Yep, it's right. But, nope. Nothin' else."

He turned one of the knives so the handle was toward Jacob. The bounty hunter looked from the knife to the man and back again.

"Over there," Fitz said, gesturing with a nod. "As long as you're chopping, I'm talking."

Jacob glanced to where the big man indicated and saw a tall pile of yellow onions spilling over the workspace. "I can do that," he said, taking the knife from Fitz.

The cook followed him to the far table, and set a big pot down heavily. "Fill this. What else you want to know about Slippery?" He patted Jacob heartily on the shoulder before crossing to the other table crammed in the small space. He lit a fire and set a pot to warming.

The bounty hunter thought about how to word his questions as he sliced the first onion in half; the pungent stench stung his eyes. Jacob had always had a more sensitive nose than most people, but he pushed past it. "How long ago were you with the gang?"

"I told you. I never was *with* the gang. Slippery just brought me on to cook for them. I always stayed back at the camp minding my own business while they went about theirs." The big man started tossing flour, butter, eggs and Jacob couldn't tell what else into a big bowl. He mixed vigorously as he answered questions.

"How'd you find yourself in that position, then?" Jacob eyes continued to water as he chopped.

Fitz shrugged. "Didn't have nothing else to do. Hooked up with Slippery round about El Paso. I had been there for a few weeks, making my way cooking for a cathouse, when Slippery came in. He liked my onion soup and my rhubarb pie and made me an offer. That town was getting too hot for me to handle, as it happens, so I accepted."

"When was this?"

"Oh, let's see." Fitz scratched at his neck under his beard. As he thought, he scooped of what looked like dough from a covered clay pot into the bowl he had been stirring. "Must be nine or ten months ago now. After El Paso we came farther west. Stoppin' here and there as his business required, you understand."

Jacob wanted to ask more about Stone's business. There was, of course, the delicate matter of not wanting to accuse this man of involvement unfairly.

"And you were with him for six months or so?"

"Right. Right about that, yeah. I left because one of— well, actually two of Slippery's guys were getting out of hand. Brothers. They'd keep going off on their own, making more trouble for the gang."

"You included?"

"Hell yes," Fitz said emphatically. He sprinkled a handful of flour on the tabletop and upended the bowl he had been mixing. A mound of dough sat waiting to be handled. "Those goddamned Maloneys. Always thinking they were smarter than everyone else. So, a couple months ago, the brothers set to stealing a barnful of horses, and ended up killing the kid who got in their way. Couldn'ta been more than ten years old and just wanted to keep his gelding. Slippery made amends to the parents as much as he could, but I wasn't having any more of it. I don't want to be feeding men like that. They ain't going to be roving around the countryside with my help. So I lit on out of there. Olmos wasn't my first stop, but this is where I managed to find me a proper job. The owner here was more than happy to look the other way when I told him where I come from."

Jacob listened to this story with interest. He had never pegged Elliott "Slippery" Stone as the kind of man who would make amends for another fellow's error, but if Fitz was to be believed, he did it without complaint. But Stone's behavior wasn't the only part of that story that grabbed his attention.

"Did you say Maloney brothers? Two of them? Was one of them named Seamus by any chance?"

"How'd you know that?" Fitz asked, narrowing his eyes at Jacob. "He get mixed up with the law again?"

Jacob dumped several handfuls of chopped onions into the pot before answering. "Were you very close to Seamus Maloney?" he asked, trying to be casual.

"Seamus? No. Not particularly. He was a mean son-of-a but manageable. If Colin weren't around Seamus might have been a better part of the gang."

"Hm," said Jacob, noncommittally. "So it was these boys that drove you to leave the gang? Any hard feelings with Stone?"

"Nah. He understood. Real understanding man, that one. He's a real leader. Not what you'd expect of an outlaw but . . . " Fitz shrugged. "I suppose it ain't strictly true to say he's a 'good' man, but he certainly could have been worse. Why is it you need to know all this stuff, eh?"

Jacob weighed his next words carefully. Could he trust this man? He had, after all, been part of the Slippery Stone Gang, hadn't he?

"Here," Fitz said walking over to where Jacob was still chopping onions. "Try this for me. I think it needs more somethin' . . . pepper, maybe."

He held out a small bowl with a few spoon-fuls of soup in it. Jacob took it from him, raised the spoon to his lips and swallowed a mouthful. The mellow scent rounded out to a sharp, bright taste. The sweet onions Jacob had been chopping seemed destined for another batch of this.

Impressed, he looked back up at Fitz. "Is this the onion soup Stone hired you for? I think it's perfect. Where'd you learn to cook like that?"

"Army," he said shortly. "Confederates. Had to make do with practically nothing."

"You did God's work then, my friend," Jacob said with a grin, handing back the bowl. "I was a Confederate myself and if I had tasted anything this good I could have beaten the entire Union Army single-handedly."

Fitz laughed and returned to his soup pot over the fire. The two men worked in silence for another moment before Jacob spoke up again.

"We got word that we should expect Stone and his gang to hit the bank across the street here. Sometime before tomorrow afternoon."

Jacob glanced over at Fitz, trying to gauge his reaction. The other man tasted his soup one last time before putting the lid on the pot and moving back to the dough that needed his attention.

"Is tomorrow the last day before the stage-coach takes the money?" Fitz asked.

Jacob chuckled. "It is."

"Yep, that sounds like Slippery. Efficient as

ever. Where'd you hear about this alleged scheme?"

"One of his girls got arrested in Phoenix and talked."

"And you believe her?"

Jacob shrugged, putting another few handfuls of chopped onions into his pot. "Should we not?"

"Couldn't really say. Depends on which girl. Depends on what she knows." He shrugged. "All's I can tell you is it sounds like the kind of thing Slippery Stone would do, so you're best to assume it will happen."

"Anything else we should worry about, like tricks he might use or distractions to look out for?"

Fitz appeared to consider the question for a moment before answering. "I dunno. That's why he's slippery, ain't it? Sure, he's efficient. He'll go where the cash is. But otherwise he's completely unpredictable. Only thing I can offer you is to hope that the Maloney brothers aren't on this particular job with him."

Jacob nodded. "Thanks."

"That's plenty of onions," Fitz said, nodding to the nearly full pot next to Jacob. "That'll keep me for the rest of the day. I imagine you have a lot you need to go take care of."

He tossed Jacob a scrap of cloth to wipe his hands on. The scent of onion would follow him for a bit, but he had gotten information they could use to take down the Slippery Stone Gang.

CHAPTER SIX

When he left Fitz to his cooking and exited the saloon, Jacob realized it was now fully morning. The warm dawn light cast shadows across the dusty street, mostly still empty at this time of day. He stepped off the boardwalk and looked in both directions. Olmos was a small town, with one main road running straight through and then into the open desert at both ends. Small homes and storefronts were built off the main road, but none more than half a mile or so away.

Though it was a small town, the next closest was a day's ride. All the miners and ranchers in the area used the First Bank of Olmos when they had cash needs. The building standing across from him must have held the life savings of hundreds of families.

After looking around, Jacob realized that if they positioned themselves right they should be able to see any gang of outlaws coming in plenty of time. The First Bank of Olmos was in the center of town, easy to defend but also easy to access.

Jacob found the U.S. Marshal in the street out front of the bank talking with another man. Younger than Jacob, but with the bearing and presence of a man used to being in charge, the stranger seemed to be leading the conversation.

"Payne," Santos greeted him as Jacob approached. "Didn't think I'd be seeing you first."

"Fitz was easy to talk to. Thought you could use my help right about now. The deputies still aren't awake?"

Santos shook his head. "Guess we're getting started without them. You and me and the sheriff will have to finalize our decisions and fill the others in later."

"Sheriff Gleason," the other man said, offering his hand to Jacob. "I can't thank you boys enough for helping us out like this."

"Just doing our job, Sheriff. I'm sure the marshal told you the same thing."

"He did," the sheriff said with a chuckle. He nervously unhooked and then re-hooked the hammer loop holding his revolver in place. "Doesn't mean I'm not grateful and won't be buying you all a drink later tonight if this all works out."

"I think we can handle that," Santos said. "The sheriff has just been telling me about the layout here, what we can expect from the bank management. What we need to be wary of. A couple of the boys that work here are going to insist on helping, probably." He rolled his eyes. "I think we've got this stunt pretty well handled. Did you learn anything useful from the cook?"

Jacob nodded. "Yep, some. Mostly just confirmed that the plan sounded like something Stone would do. Fitz himself wasn't in on any of the gang's crimes directly, but heard enough."

"And you believe him?"

"I think I do. I could be wrong, though," Jacob allowed. "I've been wrong before."

"Well, you've been right enough that I'm glad you're here," Santos said. "In fact, Sheriff and I were just laying out where we need each man to be. We'll set up in our positions all day today and tomorrow just in case we're wrong about the timing."

"Seems reasonable." Jacob was already thinking about what he needed to do before then. Maybe seeing the town's doctor, just to make sure his wound was healing properly, would be prudent. He was so consumed with his plans that he almost missed what Santos said next.

"Payne, I need you to be the man inside."

Jacob blinked in surprise. "Marshal, you know I'm here to help. I'll do whatever needs doing, but have you forgotten that I'm still healing from this shot to the gut?" Jacob gestured to his side where the bulk of the bandage was easily visible under his shirt. "If things go south, I don't know that I can be the man to chase someone down or fight with my fists."

"I know," Santos said, nodding glumly. "But the fact is, Jacob, you're the only one of all of us that isn't known to Stone. My face," he gestured. "The deputies, Sheriff Gleason. All of us have almost certainly been seen by or known to Stone through our line of work."

"The man hates me," Gleason said with a laugh. "He's going to hate me even more after this job."

"You're right." Jacob readily agreed, in spite of his misgivings. "Of course. That's why I'm here. You want me inside the bank? The last line of defense."

"Exactly," Santos said. "The sheriff and I will be in our rooms across the way." He gestured to the hotel. "I'll put each of the deputies a block or so away, watching for the gang come into town."

"And the goal?" Jacob clarified.

"The aim will be to stop the gang before they even get to you," he said. "But if they somehow get passed us and into the building, we need a man there capable of taking control of the situation. A man that they won't suspect as the law when they enter. It will give you at least some modicum of surprise."

Jacob nodded. It made sense. All he had to do was be ready and trust the others to do their jobs. That he could handle, bullet wound or no.

He couldn't deny it worried him, though.

The lawmen hustled the rest of the morning to get everything in place for their ambush. But then once it was settled, all they could do was wait. The following afternoon, Jacob found himself behind the counter of the First Bank of Olmos again. As each minute passed the tension rose. The two bank employees, Thomas and Wyatt, that had volunteered to be on duty that day were restless and fidgety.

The sheriff had sent word around the town for the residents to avoid the bank at all costs that week. The manager, Mr. DeWitt who was safe at home, had grumbled about losing business for two full days, but Marshal Santos had set him straight in no uncertain terms. And while that esteemed, powerful man remained safe, Jacob had waited inside the bank fully armed and as ready as an injured man could be to defend the cash from the outlaws reportedly on their way to steal it.

And now, still waiting for something to happen, Jacob stood with his back to the wall, with a view of the entire space. From what he had seen, the bank was one of the only buildings in Olmos that could boast of large front windows. This allowed Jacob a clear view the moment the Slippery Stone Gang approached, but also put anyone near the front of the bank at risk. He rested his hand on the butt of his gun, hammer loop undone and ready.

"It'll be today, won't it, Mr. Payne?" Thomas asked. The young man had been the first to volunteer for this post. "It has to be today, doesn't it? If they're gonna come at all? Right? That's what Sheriff Gleason said. Tuesday. He told me Tuesday."

Jacob nodded slowly, trying to will calm upon the younger man. "That's my understanding. If Stone is still going to go through with the plan, it will likely be today. We can't assume anything, though, so it's best to be prepared any time."

Thomas nodded. "I know. I know. I'll just keep—"

He stopped himself shortly and looked in panic toward the windows. The sound of horses galloping up the street toward the First Bank of Olmos drowned out any further conversation.

CHAPTER SEVEN

As the sound of hooves drew nearer to the First Bank of Olmos, Jacob Payne drew his gun. He listened hard for any sound of gunshot or shouting. There should be something. If this was the attack, the defense should begin. Any moment now, the marshal or a deputy would step in to make the arrest. There were no fewer than four men outside the bank positioned to take down the Slippery Stone Gang before they even stepped foot inside the building.

Yells and indistinct commands cut the air in the street outside. The gang was approaching.

Beside him, Thomas and Wyatt stood frozen in terror. In his conversations with them over the previous day and a half, Jacob had learned that neither of the young men had been anywhere near violence or danger of this kind. He had gotten the impression that they both felt as though something was lacking in their lives, or that each was somehow less of a man because he hadn't yet been shot at. This volunteering was meant to prove something, even if just to themselves. Jacob hadn't had a chance to convince them otherwise, but maybe this whole adventure would fulfill their need.

The shouting in the street was unintelligible. Jacob couldn't tell if it was the lawmen or the outlaws shouting commands. He hopped over the counter and crept closer to the windows to see what was happening without giving anyone outside a clear shot at him.

"What do we do, Mr. Payne?" Wyatt asked in a carrying whisper, as though they hadn't already gone over the plan three separate times.

"Guns drawn. Take cover," he answered brusquely. These were grown men who should not need his protection, but if he could keep them out of the fracas he would.

Trying to peer out the windows, he realized the streaks of grime and dirt that coated the glass made it difficult to see out of. He could roughly count eight—no, nine?—horses and riders stopped outside the bank, but from this distance, at this angle, through this dirt screen it was impossible to tell for sure.

Where were the deputies? Where was the marshal? Where was the firepower that Jacob was only supposed to be the back-up of?

How had every other line of defense failed?

As that thought flitted through his brain, the sound of a shot cracked through the main street of Olmos. If he was not mistaken, that was a rifle. Mostly likely Santos's rifle shot from his window at the hotel across the street. The marshal had been keeping watch from Jacob's own room, ready to strike at the first sight of the outlaw gang. Jacob redoubled his grip on his gun and watched.

This was the moment of truth. If everything went according to plan, the other four men would have the entire situation in hand without Jacob having to lay eyes on any member of the gang.

But when had anything ever gone according to plan for him?

Jacob had crept through the bank all the way to the front, near the windows. This put him only a dozen or so feet from the front door, and when the shouting voices outside grew closer, Jacob stood his ground.

More gunshots rang out, and Jacob ducked

down below the edge of the window. More shouting. More horses galloping. A woman's scream followed by a heavy barrage of gunshots. From the other side of the counter, a small yelp drew Jacob's attention. One of the young men there in the bank was having difficulty keeping his fear to himself.

In the small moment Jacob had turned toward the back of the bank, the front door burst open. With the afternoon light, the men entering were only in silhouette—enough for Jacob to take aim, though not enough to be certain these were the outlaws he was waiting for.

"Hold it right there," he shouted, standing abruptly and aiming his revolver.

"I'll take this," one of the silhouettes said to the others.

The man strode toward Jacob, and as he closed the few feet of distance between them, the bounty hunter felt a pang of recognition. The instant passed as the man, glaring at him under thick black eyebrows, drew back and swung at Jacob with closed fist. Jacob reacted immediately—using his forearm to block the punch, while at the same time drawing up his knee into the other man's gut. The outlaw grunted, stumbled back a couple steps, but didn't fall.

"I said hold it," Jacob yelled.

The other two silhouetted men had entered the bank during Jacob's brief struggle, ignoring the bounty hunter and making their way to the counter. They headed directly to the cash and the reason they were there.

Now that Jacob could get a good look at them all, he was surprised to notice that none of the attackers had bothered to cover their faces or disguise themselves in any way. They were either exceedingly stupid or exceedingly arrogant. Jacob memorized every feature and detail as quickly as he could; they wouldn't get away with a thing.

"Give us all you got," one of the men growled at the bank employees.

Thomas and Wyatt were still taking cover behind the counter, crouched down and out of sight. Wyatt stood, shaking but still trying to hold his gun steady.

"Drop it," the outlaw said in an almost bored voice. "C'mon, kid. You don't want to do this."

Wyatt must have come to the same conclusion, because he dropped his gun without any argument.

All of this exchange occurred in the half a minute it had taken Jacob to again overpower the third man. The two focused on the money had neglected their friend, and while the black-haired man was doubled over, Jacob easily coaxed a loop of rope around him and knotted it. The man thrashed around as he realized what was happening, but Jacob had already trapped him, with his arms bound to his sides and the length of rope in the bounty hunter's strong hands.

"Gah!" the man cried. "Let me go!"

The two others turned to look at their companion, which gave Thomas a small window in which to be brave. Out of the corner of his eye, Jacob saw the young man stand up from behind the counter and aim his own gun at the outlaws.

"D-D-Drop it!" he stammered. "Drop your weapons!"

Before either of the men could react, Thomas fired. Even at such a close distance, his shot went wide, the bullet embedding in the wall behind the men. Maybe it was the surprise, or maybe it was something else, but the man who had not yet spoken dropped his own gun to the floor and put his hands above his head.

"Wyatt!" Jacob called. "Move!"

The young man cowered against the wall, frozen and watching the proceedings with wide eyes.

"You too," Jacob said to the last outlaw, pointing his gun. "You're outnumbered."

Thomas continued to aim his weapon at the outlaw with his hands up. The last holdout glared at Jacob, then looked to his comrades in frustration. He recognized the truth of the situation. Maybe he could hold out to see if any more of the gang pushed their way into the bank, but if it hadn't happened yet he couldn't count on it.

The man cursed and dropped his gun, scowling at Jacob the whole time.

"Wyatt!" the bounty hunter shouted sharply.

Now that the outlaws had dropped their weapons, the young man was able to force himself into action. With Thomas still holding his aim steady, Wyatt gathered more rope that had been stashed behind the counter of the bank and brought it forward.

"Here. I'll do it," Jacob offered.

He handed off the length of rope to the bank employee and took care of the other two outlaws himself.

The three men glared at Jacob, but he had done his duty. The bank and all its deposits were safe. The men had been stopped, incapacitated and now bound for justice.

CHAPTER EIGHT

"I think we're all set," Jacob called out as he triple-checked the knot on the ropes binding the last man's wrists together.

"Yeah, you'd better pray I don't get free," the man closest to Jacob said, before spitting in the dirt and just missing Jacob's boot.

Jacob had been interested but not surprised to learn that one of the three men he had apprehended trying to rob the First Bank of Olmos was Colin Maloney. Judging from what Fitz had said about this man, he was sure to be on the front lines of the assault on the bank. The other two members of the gang—Miller and Escobar—were both familiar to Santos, though Jacob had not yet heard of them.

Truth be told, there were so many wanted

posters in the marshal's office at any given time, it was no wonder Jacob had not yet come across these two. Far too many men doing heinous acts were rampant through the Arizona Territory. Now, fortunately, three of those men were in custody.

The deputies Lowry and Little already had their hands on the men, ready to transport them to the Olmos jail, dragging them if necessary. The three outlaws were bound individually and then to each other; they wouldn't be getting free.

"I can't thank you enough." Sheriff Gleason took hold of the third man, wrapping his hand around his upper arm. "I'm sure Mr. DeWitt and his colleagues back east would thank you as well. You sure it's okay to keep these men together tonight?"

"We'll be leaving in the morning," Santos said. "The gang can all cool their heels in the jail overnight. I'm not riding in the dark for anything."

"You're going to let me buy you a drink, aren't you, Mr. Payne?" the sheriff asked.

Jacob looked to the marshal. "Not just me, I hope. I was the last person to have any part of this. You all stopped the other half-dozen men. It was a group effort."

"Oh, the others have already agreed. Once I get these bastards booked in the jail, I'll meet you all at the saloon."

The deputies left with the sheriff; Jacob and Santos made their way into the saloon, finding two stools at the end of the bar. A quick word with the bartender and they each had a cold beer in front of them.

"Sheriff can get the next round," Santos said, as he took a big gulp.

Jacob wrapped his hands around his glass, thinking about the events of the day. He took a small drink of his own beer, allowing the two men to sit in thoughtful silence another moment before broaching the problem that had been bothering him.

"That seemed too easy, didn't it, Marshal?"

Santos looked at him in surprise. "Did it? I have to say, Payne, from where I was standing it didn't look easy at all. In fact, the great bulk of the gang got away, including the leader. No, I'd say that while we can claim success by stopping the robbery, we could have done a lot better."

"Yes, that's true," Jacob responded thoughtfully. "Only . . ."

"Spit it out, Payne. What're you thinking?"

"Regardless of how many of Stone's gang

were out there, three of those men made it into
the bank."

"Yes?"

"Three. Now, Marshal, I'm good. I know you
know that. I have no shame in saying I am likely
one of the best, most diligent bounty hunters
you got working this part of the territory. But
even I should have a problem taking down three
professional outlaws on my own in that short of
time with the resources I had."

"Now, don't be—"

"No, hear me out." He held his hand up.
"Begging your pardon, sir. But I wonder if
maybe those men wanted to get caught."

Santos laughed. "Payne. You're suggesting
that members of the Slippery Stone Gang delib-
erately let themselves be captured by a U.S.
Marshal? You do know why he's called Slippery,
don't you?"

Jacob paused before answering. Said that
way, it did sound outlandish. But so too did the
idea that men of that nature gave in as quickly
as they had. He nodded. "I think they might
have, yes."

"For heaven's sake, why would they do that?"

"I'm not sure," he answered slowly. "But you
know we are talking about the Slippery Stone
Gang. I know as well as you do that if these

men know anything it is how to get out of a tight spot. Just like every other member of the gang that rode into town with them today."

Santos took a long slow drink of his beer, draining the last drop. Jacob let him think, let him consider what was said. He would be the first to admit that he didn't have an answer. He didn't know why these men may have done this, but there was no denying it looked suspicious.

"Well," Santos said finally. "I don't know. But you might be right. We'll tell the deputies and the four of us will just need to be on guard for any tricks. At the very least, these men did try to rob a bank and need to be held accountable for those actions."

"I'm sure you're right, Marshal," Jacob said. "And I hope I am mistaken."

"Mistaken about what?" Sheriff Gleason said, as he walked up behind them. "You already started without me?"

"We got room for another," Santos said. He moved over one seat, to allow the sheriff the stool in between the two others. "I'll get the bartender and Jacob can fill you in."

The sheriff turned to the bounty hunter with a confused expression. As Jacob gave him the basics of his suspicions, the deputies arrived, finding seats on the other side of Santos and beginning their own drinking for the night.

"Nah, you're wrong, Payne," Deputy Lowry said. "Those men are just stupid. Look at how they gave up in the face of that kid in the bank with you. Everyone knows a man turns to a life of crime when he ain't man enough to make it any other way. This is just the way these fellows are made. It might look peculiar or suspicious to us, but I guarantee you they're just not as clever as Stone is."

"Maybe," Jacob said, nodding, though he kept his further suspicions to himself.

Having told both the sheriff and the marshal what he thought about the three men in custody, Jacob felt his conscience was clear. He had done all he could for now. He was only supposed to be the last resort for this job anyway. Jacob told himself everything would be fine. That the ride to Tucson the next day would be uneventful. That by this time tomorrow he could be back with Bonnie, even if it was just having dinner in her cafe.

He realized he had no idea if she would be at work or not the following evening. He hated this. He hated not having her be part of his life. He hated not knowing if she was safe or even where she was. The first thing he would do when he returned to Tucson would be to check on her.

The second thing he would do would be to again give himself a few days for his bullet wound to heal better. Jacob put a hand to his side. He had had the doctor of Olmos replace the bandage that morning, but already with the intensity of the scuffle, he could tell he was just about to bleed through the cotton. He'd have to have that taken care of.

"Have you, Jacob?" the sheriff asked.

He shook his head, slightly, surprised to be spoken to. His mind had been back in Tucson with Bonnie and he had forgotten where he was for a short while.

"I'm sorry, you lost me there. Have I what?"

"Have you had any other dealings with men of the Slippery Stone Gang?" Sheriff Gleason asked. "I know they seem to be spreading all over the territory, but they also seem to be better at evading the law than most."

Jacob nodded. "I have. Or, at least, to my knowledge, men that had been part of the gang at one point in time or the other. Only Stone himself knows who all he associates with. Haven't ever tussled with him directly, though."

"Me either," Sheriff Gleason said. He drained the rest of his beer and got the bartender's attention. "Whiskey? I think events of today call for whiskey."

"Are we celebrating or mourning?"

"Both, I think."

The bartender laid out a row of shots for the lawmen. One after another they imbibed the woodsy, stinging spirits.

The conversation around Jacob turned to horses—Lowry had just gotten a stallion—and Jacob's thoughts wandered back to Bonnie, back to Tucson. Back to the surety of knowing who the bad guys were and what they wanted. The events of this day had unnerved him more than he cared to admit, and the fact that the others weren't taking his concerns seriously only made it worse.

But Jacob pushed down his worries, ordered another beer, and trusted in the U.S. Marshal. He would enjoy the rest of the night and think about the three men sitting in the Olmos jail in the morning.

CHAPTER NINE

The men of Tucson slept off their beer and whiskey and were ready to be back on the road not long after dawn the following morning. The small matter of transporting three men without the requisite number of horses was solved by Santos purchasing an old wagon from one of the men of Olmos. It was rough and unbalanced, jostling constantly on the uneven road, but it did the trick. The three outlaws were bound, gagged and tossed into the back of the wagon.

Deputy Little drove the wagon, with Santos leading the caravan and Jacob and Deputy Lowry following behind, both keeping an eye on the captives. They kept their stops as short as possible, only allowing for enough time to take in the bare minimum of food and water required for the day.

As they rode, as Deputy Lowry tried to make conversation with Jacob about his stallion again, the bounty hunter's suspicions of the previous evening returned. He rode forward until he was alongside the wagon and looked at the outlaws with interest. The black-haired outlaw—Colin Maloney—had not taken his eyes off Jacob. While the other two men dozed off or stared out at the horizon without interest, Colin remained alert and glaring. When he realized Jacob was going to be riding up next to him, the outlaw sat up straighter and spoke into his gag.

"You have something to say?" Jacob asked. "Some reason you think I should listen to you?"

"Don't bother with him, Payne," Deputy Little called back from his seat at the front of the wagon. "That one has been ornery all day. He don't need any more attention."

Jacob didn't respond, but looked at Colin with interest. Especially considering what Fitz had shared with him about this man, Jacob wondered how such a ruthless person could have allowed himself to be captured so easily.

"If I take that gag off," he said, "you'll need

to answer some questions for me. How does that sound?"

Colin glowered from beneath his heavy black eyebrows, but after a moment nodded.

"All right then," Jacob said, still riding alongside the wagon. "C'mere."

The outlaw inched his way as close to the side of the wagon as he could and leaned toward Jacob. The bounty hunter pulled down the gag and was rewarded with a string of cursing that would make the most battle-hardened soldier blush.

Jacob merely waited him out. If the man actually had something he wanted to communicate, he'd get to it eventually. In so many cases with men like this, simple patience was enough to tip the scale in the law's favor. The longer Jacob failed to give him a reaction, the angrier Colin grew until he finally lapsed into silence.

After a long moment of quiet, Jacob finally spoke.

"You through?"

"You motherf—"

"As I said, Mr. Maloney," Jacob interrupted, "I removed your gag in order to ask you some questions. You ready for that or should we put it back on you?"

"What do you want?" he grumbled.

"What happened to the rest of your gang once you three were inside the bank?"

Whatever question Colin had been expecting, this wasn't it. He pulled back a little in surprise before blurting out, "Nothin'!"

"Nothing? Come on, now. The deputies saw a whole crowd of men just ride away, taking your horses with them. Why would they do that when they had no clue what was happening inside the bank?"

"You'll have to ask them once you catch them, huh, Jacob Payne?"

Jacob frowned. "You know my name?"

Colin looked smug, smiling with lips closed tight.

"All right then," Jacob said. "Another question. I thought you boys were professionals. Why were we able to take you in with just an injured bounty hunter and a couple scared kids?"

"Just not my day, I guess," Colin said with a shrug. "I've always been unlucky."

"That seems unlikely."

"What can I say? The big, strong, invincible Jacob Payne outsmarted me."

Jacob didn't like the venom the other man had injected into the word invincible. Though it had only been a few days since it had happened, it occurred to Jacob that maybe Colin knew he had been the one to kill his brother Seamus. With the right connections, under the right circumstances, word could have spread to the Slippery Stone Gang already. He debated with himself whether to come out and ask the man, but decided against it.

"One more question. Where's Stone now?"

Colin laughed, just a small chuckle at first, before it developed into a full-blown cackle. He had trouble catching his breath, he was laughing so hard. Tears streamed down his cheeks, but with his hands bound, the outlaw couldn't wipe them away.

Jacob knew the man was laughing at him, but he didn't care enough about what he thought to mind the mocking. The bounty hunter was—had always been—on the right side of the law and a little laughter wouldn't deter him.

He didn't bother to put Colin's gag back, but slowed his horse just enough to be riding again behind the wagon, alongside Deputy Lowry.

"Worth it, Payne?" the deputy asked with a smile. "You didn't really think he'd give you anything useful, did you?"

"You can get a lot more information from

the way a man answers you than you can from what is said. I still think these men were taken down far too easily, and nothing Maloney just said to me has swayed me from that notion."

"However we got 'em, we did get 'em. This is three less men that Slippery Stone has to do his bidding and rob other banks around the territory. We'll get these boys back to Tucson, throw 'em in jail and get a judge to take care of 'em right quick. You did good, Payne. Don't let your doubts convince you otherwise."

"Thanks, Deputy."

"You looking forward to getting back?"

"I am. Yes. I hadn't thought to take any jobs this week. Glad I could be there to help this time, but I do need to give myself at least a few days to rest. This bullet wound is nothing less than aggravating."

"Rest. Heal. Court your girl. I get it," the deputy said with a grin.

"That's also a priority, yes," Jacob allowed with a smile. "Bonnie has been so supportive of all of this. If I can pay her back by being at least in the city for more than a couple days at a time, I'd like to do that."

"You're a good man, Jacob. Bonnie would be lucky to have you."

"I'm lucky to even know her, Deputy. And I intend to tell her so as soon as I can."

Jacob looked up ahead and caught the eye of Colin Maloney. Had he overheard their conversation? The anger evident in his face made Jacob almost certain that the outlaw had heard the details of his brother's death. While the bounty hunter was confident in his skills and advantage, he still found himself being grateful that the other man was bound.

Jacob counted down the hours till he was back in Tucson, away from this man and near again to Bonnie Loft.

CHAPTER TEN

Riding into Tucson after dark, all the men were in a hurry to get their captives transferred to the jail and out from under their watch. Deputy Little pulled the full wagon up in front of the building, and with guns leveled at the prisoners, the four men pulled the outlaws to the ground. They were marched inside and had their bindings and gags removed before they were shut in for the night.

Once the locked doors clicked behind them, Jacob breathed a sigh of relief at a job well done.

Putting the men in separate cells filled the jail, but Santos assured them that the judge would handle their sentencing in the next few days. They could stay put, cooling their heels till the end of the week. And if another criminal came along that also needed a jail cell in Tucson, they could deal with that then.

Jacob said his goodnights, and walked his horse Blaze through the dark streets to the livery. He was ready to be done. He had been relieved to see the back of Colin Maloney. The way the outlaw had watched him during their full day riding back to town had unnerved Jacob.

But now that the man was under lock and key, Jacob could put him from his mind and move on to the next problem. As much as he would like to believe he could easily hit the road again for another bounty, he would only be hurting himself more. He might be strong and resilient, but he would only stay that way by making prudent decisions. He'd stay put in town too, giving his wound just a few more days to heal before he put his body under strain again.

Jacob was impatient, but he was practical.

That night, he slept like the dead. It was a solid, dreamless sleep that he had needed more than he realized. When he woke the following morning, the first thing Jacob recalled was that Bonnie did not yet know he was back in town.

She would be the focus of his day.

It was still too early in the morning for Jacob to pay her a call, so he contented himself with attending to other personal matters. He hadn't had a bath in several days. He needed to clean his gun and empty his travel pack. And he had promised himself he'd treat his horse, Blaze, to a handful of carrots and an apple now that they were back from another hunt. That animal was his right hand when he was on a job and deserved the best.

As Blaze munched on his second apple in the livery, Jacob stroked the horse's neck absentmindedly and pulled out his pocket watch. It was mid-morning by now, late enough that Jacob could seek out Bonnie without appearing overeager. Not that he minded if she knew he wanted to see her, but he didn't want to take up too much of her time.

He said good-bye to Blaze and headed back toward the center of town. He was closest to the cafe, and though he didn't know if Bonnie would be there today, he had to check. When he ducked his head in, Mrs. Everill greeted him cheerily.

"Mr. Payne, you're back! We're so pleased to see you."

"Thank you, ma'am." He continued to look

around the room for a sign of his sweetheart, but didn't want to appear rude to the older woman.

"I don't see any new bandages," she teased. "You seem to have gotten through another adventure unscathed."

"I did, ma'am, yes. Everything is under control." He peered over her head to the open door of the kitchen, but didn't discern any movement.

"You wouldn't be looking for Miss Loft, would you?"

Jacob grinned. "Might be. Is she here?"

"Not yet, Mr. Payne. I'm expecting her in an hour or so. You're welcome to stay—"

—But Jacob was already on his way out the door. If Bonnie wasn't there he didn't need to be either.

"Thank you, Mrs. Everill," he called cheerily.

The last thing he heard as he exited was her chuckling at him.

He bounded up the steps to the front door of Bonnie's boarding house and knocked firmly. He all but bounced on the balls of his feet, anticipating seeing her again, talking to her, learning about how she had spent the last few days. When the door opened, he knew he already had a wide smile on his face. Bonnie herself had answered the door; Jacob was grateful for the short reprieve from her landlady's disapproval.

"Jacob," she said in surprise. "You're home."

"For a few days at least."

She looked him up and down, studying him in the same way Mrs. Everill had. "You're uninjured?" she asked anxiously.

"The previous wound still smarts a bit, but no new injuries. I'll stick around town for another few days to be sure of it."

She smiled, teasing him. "I've heard that before."

"I know. You're right." He restrained himself from taking her hand in his. "But I've told the marshal the same. I'm not really sure they even needed me this last time."

"I'll get some lemonade and you can tell me all about it. Make yourself comfortable," she said, gesturing him to the rocking chair on the porch.

He sat, resting his hands on his knees, and tried to relax. The morning sun was serene, and the street Bonnie lived on was quiet and comfortable. He could see why she liked living here. The moment she stepped back onto the porch with a pitcher and two glasses, Jacob felt his whole body sink into the chair. He was calm. This was where he needed to be.

Bonnie poured them each a glass of cold, sweet lemonade, and prompted him with a question. With her as the adoring audience, Jacob blossomed into a storyteller. His descriptions of Fitz, of W. Henry Ferguson, and of Sheriff Gleason brought these men to life for her. His tale of capturing the outlaws made her gasp with worry, and ask the same questions Jacob himself had been asking. Bonnie's feedback helped him appreciate what he had done even more, and made him proud to be a man of the law.

She listened attentively, until a full hour had passed. Bonnie stood up, taking the nearly empty pitcher with her.

"Jacob, I'm so sorry, but I have to be getting to the cafe."

"I'll walk you there," he offered as he stood. "Let me carry your apron or your—"

"I'm fine, Jacob," she said with a laugh. "Really."

She entered the house leaving him on the porch to wait. And wait he did, determined to see her to her next destination. He had only just got back; he wasn't going to give up even five minutes he could be spending with her. When she returned to him, she had changed into an old dress, and had her apron in hand.

"You don't have to do this," she said, smiling at him. But she did hand him her apron which he tucked under one arm, while offering her his other elbow.

"I want to," he assured her.

"Thank you," she said demurely, taking it. "I'd be happy to have company between here and there."

The walk to the cafe was just as soothing as the past hour on her porch had been. She told him about the turkeys her neighbor had just acquired and the quilt she had started the day before, all the things he had missed in town while he was gone. He offered to meet her that night to walk her home again and she accepted. Jacob could get used to this. He could easily fill every day he was in Tucson with moments just like this.

The problem became that he never knew how much time he would be spending in Tucson. He hated to keep her waiting for him, but as of yet she hadn't seemed to mind.

"I'm glad you're back, Jacob," she said.

"I am too. Now that I am, I am hoping to be able to accompany you to church this Sunday. Would that be all right?"

"There isn't anything I'd like more." Bonnie beamed at him.

CHAPTER ELEVEN

Jacob tore himself away. He had enjoyed every moment of walking Bonnie to the San Xavier Cafe, and he had secured seeing her the coming Sunday. This was exactly how he had wanted to spend his first day back in town. But now she had to focus on her work. Someday, maybe soon, he could give her a home and support so she wouldn't have to work. But until that happened he would support her as much as he could, which sometimes meant drinking cup after cup of coffee.

But as much as he wanted to, Jacob wouldn't let himself spend all day just watching Bonnie wait tables. That wasn't the rest that he needed to do. He had promised her he would rest, so he readied himself to head back to his boarding house.

Just one step out the door and he was diverted.

As he exited the cafe, Jacob was surprised to hear gunshots coming from down the street. He looked around frantically, trying to identify the source of the sound. Who could be doing that? It was the middle of the day, and everyone was out. There shouldn't be shooting going on. Someone could get hurt.

Someone might already be hurt.

And he had to stop it.

Jacob took off running toward the sounds.

After only a few steps he realized two things: he was running toward the jail and the number of gunshots had increased, accompanied by angry yelling. Jacob ran faster toward the noises, holding a hand to the bandage on his side as he felt the still-healing muscles strain with the exercise.

Jacob rounded the corner onto Court Avenue and found himself only blocks away from complete chaos.

At first glance he couldn't even tell what was happening, only that there were more than a dozen men in the street—fighting, pushing, shooting, screaming. Horses kicked up dust as they ran loose about the mob, some guided by riders but others simply on their own. Jacob continued to run, though he slowed as he grew closer to the mess, unsure what he could do or who he could help.

If this was happening anywhere near the jail, he needed to find the marshal.

As Jacob tried to wrap his brain around what was happening, he realized that most of the men in the horde wore kerchiefs and scraps of cloth over their faces. He couldn't identify any of them. All masked strangers. All congregated outside the Tucson jail.

Jacob felt his stomach drop; he hated to put words to what he was seeing.

It couldn't be a coincidence that the day after they capture three members of the most notorious outlaw gang in the territory, a larger posse of masked men appear wreaking havoc outside the Tucson jail.

There appeared to be at least ten or so men pushing themselves through the doorway into the jail. Whoever was on the other side of the door held his own, but Jacob could see that the throng would soon be able to break through. On either side of the jail, and across the street, the other dozen men were breaking everything they could get their hands on—from the front window of the dry goods shop to the sacks of flour in their back storeroom.

Goods, furniture, pills and tinctures from the pharmacy were already strewn about the street. The wife of the pharmacist—Mrs. Bart —sat dejectedly on the boardwalk twenty feet from her family's store, sobbing into her hands.

Mr. Hansen, the dry goods storeowner, pulled on the arms of one of the outlaws, trying to rip the bolt of cloth from his hands. His face was nearly purple with anger as he shouted at the men destroying his livelihood. Across the street, immediately next to the jail, was a small school. It seemed as though the outlaw gang had no regard for the security of children either. Broken slates and loose paper nearly covered the boardwalk in front of the building.

All the damage and chaos that filled the streets served to distract from their true aim— which Jacob now suspected was access to the captives that had been brought in the previous night.

Quickly scanning the crowd, Jacob identified Tucson residents, neighbors and Good Samaritans trying to help, but none of the lawmen he needed. There must be someone on the other side of that door, but were they all there?

Was Jacob on his own?

He realized he had stopped running with still a block to go. The bounty hunter paused a minuscule moment to choose his path, and then set off running again.

He had to protect the jail.

As he ran, Jacob released the hammer loop and drew his revolver. Fortunately, in his chores that morning, he had made time to clean the gun and reload it completely. He was as ready as he could be with the injury he still sported. For a brief moment he considered covering his own face with a cloth to try to blend in with the outlaws, but they had already spotted him.

Jacob threw himself into the throng, gun leveled, throwing elbows and pushing his way to the door of the jail.

"Get back!" he cried. "All of you!"

Only a tiny fraction of the men even noticed him, and those two seemed to be laughing at him.

Jacob grabbed the shoulder of one of the men and spun him around. "Get away from the jail," he commanded, pushing the muzzle of his revolver directly into the man's chest.

Over his mask, the man's eyebrows furrowed. He pushed Jacob aside and continued shoving his way toward the closed door.

The bounty hunter was now in the middle of the group of men pushing their way toward the jail. He had his gun out, held above his head, and he continued to shout commands but they ignored him completely. He felt the muscles of the man behind him press into his back, giving no regard to Jacob standing there. He was simply carried along with the tide of bodies bearing down on the door.

There were so many men, so much disregard for safety or space, that at one point Jacob was lifted completely off his feet by the pressure of the crowd around him. That brief moment was the only time in his life Jacob could recall feeling completely helpless. He was a huge man, over six feet tall, and he had never before been physically overpowered in that way.

His hand was still over his head, holding his revolver. He fired indiscriminately toward the sky, hoping for a reprieve from the crowd around him.

They paused, then pressed forward even harder. From his vantage behind the first row of men, Jacob could see that they were almost through the door of the jail. Evidently, when efforts to force it opened had failed, the outlaws resorted to simply pulling apart the wood. Someone had brought an ax. Someone else was strong enough to rip out nails. Between all of them, they were slowly but surely getting through to the jail.

Jacob closed his eyes and said a brief prayer for whoever was on the other side of that door. They would be in danger no matter how they reacted or how soon Jacob could reach them. In that brief instant, a cheer went up from the crowd and Jacob opened his eyes to see the men rushing through the new break. As they all rushed in, Jacob was shunted to the side and managed to escape the stream of bodies.

He had yet to stop a single one of them.

His anger rising, Jacob grabbed at the man passing him. The stranger blinked at him before pushing back and heading into the jail. Even from out in the street, Jacob could hear the shouting, cheering and clanging coming from inside the jail. There was no mistaking it now.

This was a jailbreak.

And Jacob had to stop it.

CHAPTER TWELVE

As soon as Jacob realized that he was witnessing an attempted jailbreak, his mind started whirring on all the resources and possibilities before him. What could he use, what were his options, if he was going to be able to stop this from happening? He prayed that someone—anyone—had sent word to the marshal. Jacob couldn't stop a dozen men on his own, but hopefully help was on the way.

The noises from inside the jail grew louder. Several heavy thuds. A gunshot. The mob sounded like they were cheering. Whatever they were attempting seemed to be successful. Jacob darted inside to do what he could to stop it.

Some light poured in from the open door,

illuminating the crumpled figure in the corner. The group of men had moved farther into the building, but Jacob rushed to the man's side, recognizing Deputy Little. The man grasped his left shoulder. Jacob saw a dark, damp patch where a bullet wound had bled through the deputy's shirt.

"Deputy?" he said.

"Jacob?" He blinked, his eyes seemingly unable to focus. "Jacob."

"Are you hurt anywhere else?" the bounty hunter asked. He tore a strip of fabric from the bottom of the man's shirt to wrap around the bullet wound.

"My head," he croaked. "They slammed me in the head with something. Might've been a piece of wood from the door." With a nod, the deputy indicated the wide, broken beam lying on the floor near him. "I blacked out. Jacob, I—"

"It's okay, Deputy," he said, trying to reassure him. "We'll get you fixed up. I'm sure you did your best."

"No!" Deputy Little let go of his wound and clasped Jacob's forearm with his bloody hand. "Jacob, the keys! I think they took the keys."

Utter panic broke in a wave over Jacob's body.

"No," he whispered. "No . . ." He visually searched the deputy, patting his pockets, checking the floor all around him. "Were they on you? Were they in the desk?" He grew more frantic, backing up from the corner where the deputy lay and searching all around.

No sooner had he stood up, then he heard a triumphant cheer coming from the hallway where the jail cells were. The tell-tale jingle of a keyring met his ears, clear as day, cutting through all the other sounds the raucous group of men were making.

He thought quickly as the footsteps headed his way.

"Do you still have your gun?" he asked Deputy Little.

The prone man shook his head miserably.

Jacob looked around. He was in the office of the jail, his back against the wall, an injured man at his feet and only a small desk between him and a potentially murderous mob. In that split second he realized he didn't want to be cornered in that small room. He had to get out. If he had any chance of stopping the outlaws, he couldn't allow himself to be hemmed in that way.

As Jacob made his way back out to the street he realized that in the chaos most of the gang had poured into the jail. This left the street nearly deserted. Only Mrs. Bart and Mr. Hansen remained trying to clean up the mess that the outlaws had left behind.

Jacob had only a few moments to formulate his plan. Where was the marshal? Where was the other deputy? Could Jacob even hope to subdue a gang of this size on his own?

With gun leveled at the doorway, Jacob stood in the street and faced down the group of outlaws about to exit. If he shot once, the rest of them would shoot back. Even if he somehow managed to get off all six of his shots and take down six of the men, there would still be more to take their place. He wouldn't survive it.

And yet, he couldn't just let them walk away with the prisoners.

The first masked man exited the jail. He was short and thin, with his hat pulled low over his eyes. So much of his face was obscured that Jacob had no inkling whether or not he had seen him before.

"Stop!" the bounty hunter demanded. "Stop right now."

A second man exited the jail, striding through the street toward Jacob. A third man, and a fourth who appeared to be maybe the prisoner Escobar, though with a mask now covering his face.

"Stop!" Jacob yelled louder. "You have no right to free these men."

He pointed the gun, but with no real hope of accomplishing his aim. Jacob was failing. He was outnumbered and outgunned, and all he could do was yell fruitlessly.

"Stop now!" he yelled again.

But the masked men kept coming. One by one they stepped through the open doorway, into the dirt and toward Jacob. He kept his gun aimed, but without any real threat behind it. He still hoped to escape this attack with his life, if nothing else.

Jacob backed up several steps as the crowd approached him. With so many men against him, he found himself cornered again, despite the fact that he was outside.

Before he could run or make another move, one of the masked men approached him, right up close to him, his eyes above the mask flat and cold.

The man hauled back and punched Jacob hard across the face.

It took all of the bounty hunter's willpower to tamp down his immediate reflex—to shoot. He wanted to shoot back, to defend himself, but he'd be bringing a storm of bullets back upon himself. He clutched his revolver, but took the punch.

One man after another stepped up, surrounded him. Each man punched Jacob—in the face, shoulders, the gut. Jacob Payne was a strong man, a capable man, but even he couldn't defeat more than a dozen men at once all set on tearing him down. Blow after blow landed, bruising his muscles, breaking his nose. One of the men must have been wearing a ring of some kind—Jacob felt a cut sear across his temple and blood ran down his face.

He stayed on his feet as long as he could, but soon the gang of outlaws was continuing to pelt him even as he lay in the dirt.

He had lost. Jacob Payne had lost.

Fortunately, for him the focus of the mob's action was not to destroy him. As soon as it was clear he was no longer a threat, the group of men moved away from him, down the street and following the leadership of one of the others.

Jacob blinked through the blood in his eyes at the man who seemed to be in charge. Even from this distance, he could spot the ice-blue eyes penetrating from above his mask.

Jacob recognized those eyes.

Elliott "Slippery" Stone was here in Tucson.

Stone was in Tucson and he was leading a jailbreak, freeing three of his men.

Blows and kicks continued to rain down on him and the gang leader disappeared from Jacob's view.

"Leave him," a cold voice said. "He's mine."

As Jacob tried to pull himself to his feet, to see who was speaking, the sharp toe of a boot landed directly in the bullet wound in his side. Jacob groaned, the pain so bad that for a moment he felt like he might vomit. He closed his eyes and lay with his face in the dirt.

CHAPTER THIRTEEN

A harsh whistle cut through the air. The crowd surrounding Jacob, beating him and keeping him crumpled on the ground, dispersed without any word. The bounty hunter knew he had lost and hated himself for it. With his face still in the dirt, he groaned and moved to get up. Maybe he could still recapture one of the escaped outlaws. If he could—

"Stay down," the cold voice said, kicking Jacob's arm and knocking him back to the ground. "I'm in charge now and the great bounty hunter Jacob Payne is going to have to listen to someone else for a change."

Jacob realized why the voice sounded familiar. It was Colin Maloney. Why he was sticking around the street outside the jail instead of escaping town when he had the chance, Jacob had no idea. He blinked through the sweat and blood running down his face and looked down the street. The crowd of men all seemed to be mounting their horses and leaving town.

All but this one, bent on causing Jacob pain.

"You'll never get away with this Maloney," Jacob said with a groan. He didn't dare try to get up again. If he stayed still enough, maybe the outlaw would hold off kicking him again right away.

The man laughed. "I already have, Payne. I thought you'd realized that."

Jacob rolled over onto his back, staying on the ground but looking the outlaw in the eyes. "Not yet." He spit a mouthful of blood into the dirt by Maloney's feet.

"Why do you think it was so easy to take us back in Olmos?" he said with a smirk. "You're not that good. We're not just going to *accidentally* walk into your grasp. You played directly into my hands."

"You wanted to get caught?"

"That is exactly what I wanted."

Jacob frowned. Even though he had suspected as much, it was still hard to believe. "Why?"

Maloney laughed. "I wanted to get to you. I know who you are, Jacob Payne."

"I'm just a bounty hunter. All I do is help the law around here."

"You're a fiend. A low life who kills for money. No better than Slippery Stone or any member of the gang."

"That's absurd." Jacob was still practically under Maloney's heel, but even so he couldn't listen to such insults without defending himself.

Maloney didn't let him continue. He kicked Jacob in the shoulder, hard, again with the point of his boot. The man who had until that point withstood bullet wounds, blows and wild horses without more than a stifled groan, now cried out in pain. He felt a pop, and an intense spike of pain. His shoulder had popped out of place; he couldn't move his arm. He couldn't put weight on it and lay writhing in the dirt once more.

Maloney chuckled darkly and said, "And I know it was you that murdered my brother."

"Your brother had every chance," he said through clenched teeth. "He knew he was wanted, and he fought me rather than face justice."

Maloney kicked Jacob in the hip. "You killed

him. And now I'm going to make sure you suffer even more before you die, too."

Jacob closed his eyes. He knew it had been too easy to bring in these three men from the bank in Olmos. That had never felt right. But even so, to think that it was all revenge, that the marshal and deputies and the citizens of Olmos had all been at risk because this one wanted Jacob . . . The thought made him sick.

He had to do something.

Jacob rolled back over onto his side, pushing away the nausea from the pain. He could get through this. He would get through this. Pain was something that would just have to wait. He couldn't move his right arm—he'd never be able to aim properly—but he could still hold a revolver.

"Jacob!" a sweet, feminine voice called out.

He felt a stab of panic. He knew that voice. He knew that woman. And though he may be falling in love with her, in that moment he didn't want to see her. The last thing he wanted was for her to be anywhere near this site. Jacob rolled slightly to look down the street, dismayed at what he saw.

The streets of Tucson were chaos.

Many of Slippery Stone's gang had rode out of town, but not all. Three or four masked men had continued their mission of looting and destroying any of the storefronts they passed as the rode down the street. Broken barrels and upturned boxes littered the boardwalk on both sides.

Jacob spotted the tall, wiry frame of Marshal Santos outside the school, trying to subdue one of the outlaws while a second attacked him from behind.

And Bonnie Loft had walked directly into this chaos.

Jacob blinked again, sure the blood and dirt in his eyes was distorting his view. From where he lay on the ground it seemed as though Bonnie was wielding a rifle, holding up with both hands, though not aiming at anyone in particular.

Jacob's heart swelled with both pride and fear. This wonderful woman came to help. Unprompted, unbidden. And far beyond any situation she was ready for. He had to pray that she could escape unscathed.

"Jacob," she called again, more frantically this time.

"Seems as though that pretty little lady needs your attention," Maloney said.

"Don't even look at her," Jacob warned. He pushed himself up on his good arm, expecting every moment for Maloney to kick him back down, but thump never came.

"Jacob," came the more desperate cry again.

Jacob got to his knees and looked up toward Bonnie, dismayed to discover the reason Maloney's hit had not landed: the man was striding down the street toward Jacob's sweetheart.

"No," he said, though he knew protesting wouldn't do anything. Louder, he yelled, "Bonnie, run!"

As he sauntered down the road, toward Bonnie, toward where there was still a horse waiting for him, Colin Maloney turned and grinned malevolently at Jacob over his shoulder.

"Now it's my turn to take something of yours," he said. He spat into the dirt and turned back to the woman.

"No!" Jacob pulled himself to his feet, agonizing with every movement. If it was only to save himself, he might give up. But Bonnie was at risk. Sweet, innocent, beautiful Bonnie Loft. And whatever code of ethics other men might have in protecting women and children, Jacob knew Colin Maloney boasted no such code.

Jacob cursed the day the Maloneys had crossed his path.

When he looked up again, the outlaw had mounted his horse and was now riding the remaining twenty feet to where Bonnie stood, still desperately clutching her rifle in shaking hands.

"Jacob!" she called again, more anguished this time.

He watched helplessly as the remaining Maloney brother lifted Bonnie up, practically dragging her onto his horse and holding her captive. The woman let out a long, piercing scream. She fought back—Jacob felt a surge of pride even as he worried. But she was no match for the outlaw. He was much stronger, much crueler, and much more ruthless than she would ever be.

Jacob stumbled forward, bruised, bleeding, his right arm hanging uselessly at his side. But still he pushed forward. He couldn't allow this man—this deranged, revenge-seeking outlaw who only wanted to hurt Jacob—to get any farther with Bonnie on his horse. Jacob passed his revolver to his left hand and took aim.

"Leave her, Maloney!"

"If you want her, come and claim her," Maloney called mockingly.

CHAPTER FOURTEEN

All of their shouting and Bonnie's ear-splitting scream had finally grabbed the attention of the other men still in the streets. Marshal Santos ran toward where Maloney had seized her and held her captive. Many of the members of the gang took the opportunity of the distraction to head out of town without repercussion.

Jacob groaned inwardly. So many men were getting away with so many crimes and there truly wasn't anything he could do about it. Not only were the original prisoners going to escape unpunished for their attempted bank robbery, but every single one of the mob who had broken them out of jail, looted the nearby business and destroyed hundreds of dollars' worth of property was gone. All they had had to do was rely on their sheer number, knowing there weren't enough lawmen in Tucson to fight back.

He continued his limping walk toward where Colin sat upon his horse. Jacob wasn't sure if he would flee with his prize, or stay to make sure Jacob suffered even more. The bounty hunter may only have a few short moments in which to rescue Bonnie.

Bonnie sat on the saddle in front of Colin, his arm wrapped lecherously around her waist and holding her in place. She had stopped calling out for him, but kept her strong, uncomplaining gaze fixed firmly on Jacob, as he made his way to her.

"Let her go," Jacob called.

Out of the corner of his eye he noticed not only Marshal Santos running to the confrontation, but one of the outlaws seemed to be heading toward Colin as well. Jacob shook his head—whoever that was would be sorry they didn't escape when they had the chance.

"It's me you want," he called to Maloney.

"Oh, I can be satisfied with this one," he said, squeezing his arm so tightly around Bonnie that she squeaked.

Maloney held his revolver against her ribs. She twisted to get away from it, but he held her tight. Even from the distance of twenty or so feet, Jacob could see her shoulders rising and lowering quickly with short breaths. She must be petrified.

"She's not part of this, Maloney!"

Colin Maloney had gotten what he had so desired. He had found a way to hurt Jacob, both physically and emotionally. The bounty hunter tried to keep his voice calm, so as not to betray how anxious he was about Bonnie's safety.

The marshal had closed the final steps and his own revolver pulled, aiming at Maloney from the other side. "Let her go, you fiend," he called. "We've got you covered on both sides. You're not getting out of this alive."

"If I'm not, then neither is she," Maloney said darkly.

Bonnie gulped, eyes wide, but didn't say anything. Her equanimity under such duress was admirable.

Jacob's revolver was held tightly in his left hand. His non-dominant hand. While he had been telling himself for years he needed to spend more time practicing his shot from his left hand, he in no way felt confident in his skills yet.

"Colin Maloney," a deep voice yelled. "That woman is not part of this."

Jacob looked around, shocked and curious

about who belonged to the new voice. The only other ally he could have guessed might appear was Deputy Lowry but that hadn't sounded anything like the man. After a disbelieving moment, Jacob realized that the outlaw he had seen earlier, the one man returning to the scene in spite of his chance to escape, had removed his mask and admonished Maloney.

The man was shorter than Jacob, but still carried himself with a presence and bearing that bespoke leadership. He had pale, icy blue eyes under a mop of curly brown hair. With his masked removed, Jacob noticed the man's square jaw covered in a light brown stubble, as though he had been on the road for a few days after a shave.

It was Stone.

Elliott "Slippery" Stone. The leader of the outlaw gang was risking his own capture to rescue an innocent woman he had never met before. Jacob was shocked into silence.

"Shut it, Stone," Maloney yelled at him. "This isn't your fight anymore."

The outlaw never took his eyes off Jacob. The bounty hunter didn't take his eyes off him either. He couldn't let himself be distracted and miss what might be his only chance to rescue Bonnie.

Whether Elliott "Slippery" Stone had been in on Maloney's plan to get caught by Jacob Payne, he couldn't say. The bounty hunter found it hard to believe that there would be anything happening in that man's gang that he didn't know about. Of course, a few moments ago Jacob would have also found it hard to believe that the outlaw would berate any of his men for any crime, let alone capturing a woman.

Regardless of how it came about, Seamus Maloney's brother had used the gang and their schemes to attack Jacob in the most personal way possible. Revenge and rage had driven each of Colin's actions over the last few days.

Jacob winced at the pain from his shoulder, as well as from the bruises all over his body. With the back of his hand he wiped the still-wet blood off of his face. He must look a sight, with the blood, dirt, and sweat smeared every which way. And yet Bonnie never once looked away.

He clutched his revolver in his left hand. Despite the pain in that arm, he held steady, aiming carefully at the outlaw. With Bonnie sitting in front of Colin, there was every reason to worry about possibly hitting her. That was the only reason Jacob hadn't fired yet. He would. He had to. But he didn't want to risk injuring an innocent himself, or risk Maloney shooting her in the ribs reflexively when the gun went off.

Jacob took two slow steps forward.

"You stay where you are, Payne," Maloney said. "You're going to watch me take what you love, just like you took from me."

"We don't have to do this," Jacob said calmly. Soothingly. "Your brother died exactly the way he chose to. He could have let himself be brought in for a trial, but he insisted on a duel. It was what he wanted. Seamus had every chance."

"Don't you let his name cross your lying lips," Maloney shrieked. "You're not fit to lick his boots."

"I'm sorry I had to kill the man. Truly. But your quarrel is with me, not with Miss Loft."

"I hope after I kill her, it breaks your heart," the outlaw said coldly.

"Maloney," Stone said in a commanding tone. "We do not kill innocent women."

The outlaw broke eye contact from Jacob, turning his attention to Stone. Whatever authority and hold the leader had over members of his gang, he had wielded in that moment, demanding Maloney's attention.

Jacob saw his chance.

In turning to give Stone his attention, Maloney inadvertently directed his horse to turn as well.

That was all Jacob needed. The tiny window of opportunity to end this.

With the slightly different angle, Jacob could get a clear shot at Colin Maloney, without putting Bonnie in the middle and with enough of a margin that he was willing to risk the shot with his less-skilled left hand.

The bounty hunter took a deep breath and held it, willing his hand to stay steady.

He squeezed the trigger.

The shot tore the air. Bonnie yelped in surprise. Santos yelled for Jacob. A rough cry of pain escaped Maloney's lips.

Only Slippery Stone remained silent. He met Jacob's eyes for a short beat, across the dirt street. Whatever disagreements or quarrels the two men might have, they came together in that moment. Neither had wanted to witness the death of an innocent woman.

Stone nodded almost imperceptibly to the bounty hunter and turned to leave.

"Wait!" Jacob called.

The outlaw glanced at him over his shoulder, before breaking into a run. Before Jacob could wrap his mind around what had just happened, the gang leader had rounded the next corner and was out of sight.

Jacob had a short moment of turmoil within himself, trying to decide if running after Elliott "Slippery" Stone was the best option. Could he just let an outlaw of that notoriety leave Tucson unpursued? But, then, could Jacob really make any kind of respectable chase in his condition?

He had to take care of himself. And Bonnie.

Only a short moment had passed, but Maloney had fallen from the saddle into the dirt, clutching his chest where the bullet had landed. His foot remained tangled in the stirrup. In the surprise of the gunshot, his horse had moved forward another few steps, dragging the injured, bleeding outlaw in the dirt by his broken leg.

CHAPTER FIFTEEN

"Get the doctor," U.S. Marshal Santos yelled out.

Two of the men who had been a block away cleaning up the rubble and detritus from looting both ran down the street following the marshal's instruction. A small crowd was gathering, some to help but most only to gawk at the action.

After a quick glance at Maloney, to ensure the man would not be getting up, Santos reached up to help Bonnie down off the horse.

"Are you all right?" Jacob asked, hurrying to her side.

She nodded, as though still numb and shocked by the entire affair.

"Miss Loft, will you please take this man to

my office?" To Jacob, he offered a more direct command. "Go with her. Sit. I don't want you moving. We'll get this all taken care of."

Jacob looked over the street at the complete mess and disaster that had resulted.

Bonnie put her arm around his waist, helping him through his limp.

He wrapped his one good arm around her, while his other hung down.

After a few feet, with no one else in hearing distance, Jacob stopped. He needed to look at her. He needed to be sure she was okay. He looked full in her face briefly before pulling her into a hug.

"I'm sorry, Bonnie," he whispered into her hair. "I'm so sorry. This is all my fault."

"Please don't say that." She pulled out of his embrace to look up into his face. "This is my fault. When I heard everything that was happening I thought I'd be able to help, but instead I just got in the way."

"No, no," he protested. "I love that you wanted to help—"

"That may be," she said gently interrupting him. "But I still mangled it up. I'm sorry. I wasn't ready for this. I thought I was, but I was wrong. I couldn't even bring myself to raise the rifle, let alone shoot it."

Jacob was quiet for a moment, pulling her into another hug while he thought.

"Would you like to learn to shoot it?" he asked.

"Yes," she answered immediately. "Please. I don't want to be a burden on anyone. I'd like to be able to do it myself."

Jacob nodded. "All right, then. We'll do that. You'll learn how to fire a rifle in case you ever need to protect yourself."

"Not until you're all healed up, though," she said with a laugh. "You told me before you'd give yourself some time off. And now look at you."

"I can barely stand."

"You can barely stand and your arm doesn't work and you still have that hole in your side," she teased. She smiled at him and softened. "Please, Jacob."

"Yes, ma'am."

"There must be some other bounty hunter in the territory, isn't there?"

"Oh, I would think so. The marshal can find someone."

"That's what I like to hear," she said.

He grinned at her and pulled her close for a kiss. Any outlaw that needed chasing would just have to wait.

Lonesome Trail

Before Jacob Payne arrived in the Arizona Territory, before he was a bounty hunter, before he learned how to survive in the desert, he had to travel west. Innocents in trouble, quirky characters and life-threatening peril are along every mile as he  passed from Virginia through Texas to the desert of Arizona.

When Jacob comes across a family that has fallen victim to horse thieves, he can't just ride on and leave them to his fate. He's not yet a bounty hunter, but Jacob Payne can still hunt down the evil-doers. Tucson will be waiting for him once he brings these men to justice.

Sign-up to download this prequel story for free from my website: **http:// atbutler.com/jp-free**

ALSO BY A.T. BUTLER

Hawke's Revenge

Loyalty's Price

———

The next book in the Jacob Payne series, *Arizona Legend* is available now!

———

ABOUT THE AUTHOR

I grew up in the southwest—California Missions, snakes and constant threat of drought weaving the backdrop of my childhood.

But it wasn't until I moved to Texas a few years ago that the magic and mythology of the American West began to seep into my soul.

I'd love to write about Jacob Payne for a long time...

If you enjoyed this book, a review on your favorite retailer would be greatly appreciated.

- A

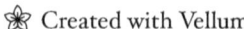